About the Illustrator

 W9-CKP-723

Name: ....

Age: .... Hometown: ....

My best friend is: ....

The most exciting adventure I've had is: ....

....

If I got to ride in Giant Kangaroo's pouch, I'd go to:

....

Me and Giant Kangaroo

COMPENDIUM®

kids

inspiring possibilities.™

This is me,

and this is Giant Kangaroo.

I sit inside Giant Kangaroo's pouch and look out at the world. "Let's go explore, Giant Kangaroo!" I say.

With a single leap, Giant Kangaroo hops over all

the houses on the street
and we're off to see the world.

We jump so fast over the
landscape it seems
like we are flying.

We go farther and higher, jumping over grassy fields and mountains and towns.

We come to a volcano with hot lava pouring down the side.

"You can do it, Giant Kangaroo!"
I say, and with one huge leap, we
go over the top and land safely.

Giant Kangaroo's feet are warm from the volcano,

so we head to the
ocean shore to cool off.

"Let's keep going, Giant Kangaroo! Can we make it across the ocean?" I ask.

Giant Kangaroo hops from island to island until we reach another continent.

The land is sandy and yellow and very warm. We made it to Egypt!

We hop over to the pyramids
to have a closer look.

The tourists at the pyramids can't believe what they see. "A giant kangaroo?" they ask each other.

They shake my hand
and take pictures of us
and share their lunch.

Giant Kangaroo and I are tired
from our long day. We take
a nap next to the Sphinx,

and then we're ready
for our trip back home.

That night, my mother tucks me into bed. "That's strange," she says, "you have sand in your hair.

How did that happen?"

WITH SPECIAL THANKS TO THE
ENTIRE COMPENDIUM FAMILY.

CREDITS:

Written by: M.H. Clark
Designed by: Julie Flahiff
Edited by: Amelia Riedler

ISBN: 978-1-935414-93-3

© 2013 by Compendium, Inc. All rights reserved. No part of this publication may be reproduced or transmitted in any form or by any means, electronic or mechanical, including photocopy, recording, or any storage and retrieval system now known or to be invented without written permission from the publisher. Contact: Compendium, Inc., 2100 North Pacific Street, Seattle, WA 98103. *Me and Giant Kangaroo*; *Story Lines*; Compendium; live inspired; and the format, design, layout, and coloring used in this book are trademarks and/or trade dress of Compendium, Inc. This book may be ordered directly from the publisher, but please try your local bookstore first. Call us at 800.91.IDEAS or come see our full line of inspiring products at live-inspired.com.

1st printing. Printed in China with soy inks. A0113030017500

COMPENDIUM®

kids

inspiring possibilities.®